TAMING THE WIND

PHILLIPA NEFRI CLARK

Taming The Wind

Copyright © 2020 Phillipa Nefri Clark

Editing by Nas Dean

Set in Australia and written in Australian English

IMPORTANT NOTE

Taming The Wind is set in Australia in 1966 & 1967. It is written in Australian/British English to provide an authentic read.

This story is a prequel to The Stationmaster's Cottage, but reads as a standalone with a happy ending.

For Nas

1

DIFFERENT SIDES OF THE SAME COIN

How wonderful to escape from Palmerston House before anyone woke, tiptoeing down the stairs (avoiding the creaky ones) and sneaking out through the door beyond the kitchen.

The cool air brushing her cheeks, Martha Ryan sprinted across the dewy lawn to the furthest corner of the property rather than follow the winding driveway to its grand gates. She scrambled over the timber fence, glancing back at the house as a light flicked on. The kitchen staff were always the first up.

When I have a home, I won't need staff.

She'd cook breakfast each day for her family. Children, at least three or four. A husband who was also her best friend. One who didn't drink too much each night with his friends and stumble home to an angry wife. The constant fights between the parents she adored were exhausting her.

On the road to the river, she picked up her pace again, longing for sand between her toes and sea spray in her hair.

At nineteen, Martha had her life planned out. A cottage overlooking the ocean. A walnut, handcrafted desk where she'd write books to sell around the world. Volunteering would be in there somewhere, helping others find their way. First though, she would travel for at least a year to distant corners of the planet.

A narrow path beside the river wove beneath a natural gap in the cliff. This was the darkest part of the route, but one Martha knew well enough to walk blindfolded. Only after a winter deluge would she avoid the shortcut, when the river sometimes swelled to dangerous levels through the narrow tunnel.

"Finally!" On the beach, she kicked off her sandals and dug her toes into cool sand with a sigh.

She wandered alongside the river until it formed a shallow lagoon before merging with the sea. The lagoon water was warm, and Martha paddled ankle-deep to the waves, which were contrastingly cold enough to make her squeal and step back. Springtime might mean daffodils and sunny days, but the Great Southern Ocean took its own sweet time to warm up enough to swim.

The tide was low and the sea calm, almost still. Martha climbed onto the old jetty as the sky lightened to her right. She loved this place but rarely got here early enough to sit alone at the end. To have it to herself for a while with no disagreements or stifling if well-meant expectations, legs dangling over, salt on her lips…what a treat.

Which might be short-lived. Martha sighed as a movement along the tideline caught her eye. A man headed her way.

Stay still. He'll keep walking. Focus on the scenery.

Martha gazed at the horizon as the colours of the sky changed. Fingers of gold and orange intermingled with the dark blue hue of the heavens. Perfect.

The old timber boards groaned under the feet of the walker. Most likely a fisherman, out for his breakfast catch so there was no point being ungracious about the intrusion. Martha planted what she hoped was a bright smile on her face and turned her head in greeting. "How gorgeous is this view?"

He'd already stopped halfway along, as though seeing her for the first time. Not a fisherman. A tiny flutter stirred in Martha despite the rather stern expression on his face. She knew him. In a town so small, everyone knew each other.

"There's room here, if you'd like to watch the day begin." She offered.

The last thing Martha wanted was him thinking it was an invitation, so she directed her attention back to the horizon. It didn't matter if he left. They'd never spoken from her recollection. Martha's friend circle was wide and eclectic, much to her mother—Lilian's—perpetual disapproval. As the region's wealthiest family, appearances mattered. At least to Lilian, and Martha's older sister, Dorothy. And Thomas Blake would certainly attract their disapproval.

Are you still there or did I scare you away?

The jetty creaked.

"Are you certain I won't be intruding?"

Martha somehow avoided jumping at his voice. Deeper than she'd imagined, although until one minute ago she'd never even thought about him. Or how his voice might sound.

"Not unless you intend to recite poetry or play bagpipes." Martha moved over a bit to make room.

He settled beside her, hands on the timber boards either side of his shorts-clad legs. "From English descent, not Scottish, so you are safe from the latter."

She snuck a glance at him. He didn't comment on the poetry.

A long silence fell, interrupted by seagulls hovering around the jetty.

Martha stared at silvery, spotted fish darting around seaweed below.

He *was* intruding. There was a presence about Thomas drawing her attention away from the sea and the sky. How had they never spoken? His father was the stationmaster and with his mother, Thomas lived in the cottage built by the Ryan family decades ago to support the train line they'd financed.

"Do you know what species those are?" Thomas nodded to the fish.

"Of course. King Whiting. *Sillaginodes punctatus.* And before you correct me, these are babies. Juveniles." Martha raised her chin.

"Do people usually correct you?"

Thomas turned his head to face her. His expression was kind. It was the only word she could summon.

"Mother, usually. Or Dorothy, when she's home. Anyway, I'm Martha."

"I know."

"Oh."

He knows who I am.

"Your parents employ my father. They own our house."

He might as well have added 'control our lives'. Martha's stomach tensed at his tone. She recognised the mix of bitterness and acceptance. It mirrored her own feelings.

Different sides of the same coin they were.

2

EXPECTATIONS

Had he allowed his discontent to show? There was a flicker of something in Martha's eyes. This was her family he spoke of. For all he knew, she was the same as Lilian and Dorothy, women who'd walked past his mother without little acknowledgement on more than one occasion. Patrick was different. Her father was a man of the people, particularly when whiskey or beer was on offer.

Thomas had expected a deserted jetty. Wanted a deserted jetty. How he treasured the time alone on its end, formulating a painting before committing it to canvas, or planning a sketch. Sometimes, like today, he'd intended to think.

Yet another discussion over dinner last night had resulted in bad feelings. Not that anyone would admit to them. Dad just grunted and left the table to go straight to bed. Always the excuse of an early start but he rose after Thomas each morning. Mum refused to let Thomas help her wash up, humming to herself as she put each plate down a little louder than necessary.

I can't be what you want.

They were good people who wanted their son to have a living. A future. Marriage to a local girl, grandchildren for them to spoil, a secure job doing what Thomas' father did, and his grandfather and great grandfather had. Stationmaster of River's End station, or more accurately, the Ryan family's timber mill train line.

"You're an artist."

Martha's voice carried no judgement of his earlier words. She sounded curious and when she smiled, his doubts of her sincerity vanished. The young woman he'd only ever seen from a distance, laughing with her friends or riding her horse along the beach, was cut from a different cloth than most Ryans.

"I am. But how did you know?"

"Everybody knows. And you were in the newspaper when you won the oil painting section at the Warrnambool arts show last year. Such a beautiful painting of the river."

A warm flush rose from Thomas's neck to his forehead and he dropped his head. "Thanks." Little more than a mutter. "My mother entered it without telling me. Never should have won."

"Yet, it did. She must be proud of you."

Debatable. Probably. But Mum always sided with Dad. Even when his own father destroyed... Thomas shook his head. What happened those years ago was in the past.

"I'd love my mother to be proud of me. She disapproves of almost every choice I make and in the same breath, reminds me how Dorothy is fulfilling her destiny." Martha stretched her toes down to touch the surface of the water. It was a bit too far. "So, I agree and make my plans to escape."

"To follow your sister to Melbourne?"

"My goodness, no! She is welcome to get a degree in business and return to take over from Father and make the business great again. Except..." Martha leaned toward him, her long hair dropping forward to brush against his arm. "I suspect Dorothy is fond of a young man in the city and may never return."

Martha sat back and gazed at the sea, oblivious, it appeared, to the effect she'd had on Thomas. His heart thudded, and his skin tingled where her silky hair strands had touched him.

He wanted to paint her, here at the end of the jetty. In her white dress, dark brown hair glistening under the rising sun, face animated with a joy of living he'd never seen in another person. How though would he, the lowly son of a stationmaster, capture the beauty radiating from Martha?

"I have to go home." She was scrambling to her feet and Thomas stood. "We have a dinner party tonight and Mother expects me there all day helping prepare."

"Is it what you want to do?"

She wrinkled her nose. So cute.

"Not when it's for stuffy businessmen. But these men order the timber and keep the line running which puts food on the tables of many families in River's End."

Said casually, the message was clear, and it stung. The Ryan family *were* this town. Martha's home—Palmerston House—stood for more than a show of wealth. It served as a reminder of how much the simple people of the region owed to one powerful family.

Martha wasn't his to paint. Or share dreams with. Or anything other than nod to as they passed in the street.

"Are you coming?"

Thomas blinked. What had he missed?

With a laugh, Martha grabbed his hand and tugged. "Let's go and splash in the lagoon like kids before going back to the real world."

3

TO LOVE THE COMMON THINGS

Thomas haunted Martha's thoughts for days. Their paths hadn't crossed again, not since laughing their goodbyes after spending far too long in the lagoon. Somehow her sandals had fallen into the deepest part of the water and her attempts to retrieve them resulted in two soaking wet people.

"Whatever are you smiling at, Martha?" Lilian carried a basket of flowers into the kitchen as Martha finished a late breakfast.

"Those are pretty."

"True. But not an answer."

"Sorry. I was just thinking about someone I met the other day. A new friend." Martha took her plate to the sink and turned on the tap.

"For goodness sake, child, we have staff to do that."

"And I have two perfectly useful hands." She kept her tone pleasant although they'd had this discussion so often it was like playing a record.

Lilian wasn't impressed. "Who is this new friend? You don't seem to spend much time with Bess and Annette lately."

"They are both travelling, Mother." Martha carried two vases to the table and helped Lilian sort the flowers as she'd done since childhood. "Off to London. Then France. They intend to find husbands. Minor royalty, if you would believe them."

"Better than the slim offerings here. Not one suitable match between River's End and Melbourne for young ladies of good upbringing."

Thomas Blake was a suitable match with his keen intellect and kind eyes, sense of humour and movie star looks. And talent. Nothing as appealing as pure talent. Martha pushed the thought away.

"You do know we live in the 1960s, not 1860s. The days of marriages based on perceived equal status are long gone." Martha breathed in the heady scent of a string of white jasmine. "I love these."

"You, my daughter, love the common things." If there was a slight smile on Lilian's lips, it didn't linger. "Jasmine is found everywhere around here. Same as the people. And stop deliberately misunderstanding me, Martha. The world requires all types from the lowliest workers to the royalty you mentioned. Everyone has their place."

"You just think my friends belong in a different place to me." Martha left the flowers to Lilian and washed her hands.

Lilian folded her arms. "You refuse to accept the generous offers from prestigious universities because you insist on a study break, but all you do is waste time with girls from the town or sit in your room."

"In my room I write stories. And you've made it clear you won't support my preference to pursue the arts. I'm still going to be a famous author, Mother."

"With nothing to fall back on. Why not be a teacher? Or nurse? Or even go into business like your sister?"

"Oh, for goodness sake, even Dorothy doesn't really want a business degree."

"Rubbish. She's a natural and loves learning."

Loves not being here. Dorothy wanted to be an opera star.

Martha needed fresh air. "I might walk into town. Do you need anything?"

"I'd like to continue this discussion, young lady."

"I'll think about being a teacher, okay?" Martha snapped.

Anything to settle Mother down and get some space. After

throwing on jeans and T-shirt and tying her hair into a ponytail, Martha stomped out via the front door. She had no destination in mind and let her feet be in charge until her temper cooled. The sky threatened rain, but she didn't care.

Not wanting to run into anyone she knew—which meant almost every person in River's End—she skirted around the township along the road hugging the cliffs. Instead of turning to the beach at the river, she went the other way and crossed the bridge. This led to the main street out of town toward Melbourne.

Only how many hours away?

The city didn't interest her. She'd spent her high school years at a boarding school there. Dorothy adored Melbourne and would never move back home, no matter how much Mother pressured her.

At the top of the hill, the last of the bad feelings drained away and Martha wandered into the tiny graveyard. For a while she visited the resting places of her ancestors, all the way back to Eoin Patrick Ryan, who'd died in 1893. He was the first Ryan to live in Palmerston House after winning it in a game of poker.

She stared over the town. A couple of streets of shops. Two or three blocks of homes in large gardens. With a population of less than four hundred, nobody built too close to anyone else. There was one school, catering for primary and high school students. How she'd wanted to stay there after primary school instead of leaving her friends behind. At least now she was back with them, particularly her closest friend, Frannie. One more thing to upset Lilian.

Rain began. It wouldn't amount to much, but she'd rather stay dry until the squall passed. Stone steps led to the beach and she hurried down to the sand in an increasing shower. On one side of the steps, the smooth, sheer cliff rose to the graveyard. On the other and a little further along was a cave. Well, an alcove really, a natural indent large enough to wait in.

The entry was filled with an artist's easel complete with canvas. And artist.

4

HIS TO TAME

Should have known this would happen.

Rain and oils don't go well. Before the first drop hit his arm he had to move from the perfect position against the cliff. He'd scoped this angle for days, picturing the finished canvas before doing as much as selecting a palette. Only two hours into painting, he'd glanced at the sky, aware of the shift in the atmosphere heralding a downpour.

The alcove would do for a while. Although not deep, it kept the canvas and paints dry and let him take a breather. With high tide approaching and under the greyish sky, the sea was a myriad of colour and movement. Each wave rolled in with a little more power, whooshing up the sand to deposit foam and treasures from its depths. All he wanted was to capture even one element to his satisfaction.

He ran a hand through hair overdue for a cut. Between his art and working in the local pub, time was precious, so appearances came last. Even his stubble was becoming a beard.

The ocean invited him to swim, or better yet, surf. A bit on the wild side, unpredictable, and his to tame.

"Oh. Um. Hi."

Martha hesitated outside the alcove, rain dripping down her face.

Uncertainty in her expression surprised Thomas and he stepped back. "There's room. Come out of the weather."

Still, she waited, biting her bottom lip.

"Martha. Are you always soaking wet or is it only when we meet?"

Her eyes lit up and she smiled, sliding past him to get under cover. "Thanks. And no, I don't live my life perpetually looking like something straight out of the sea."

Thomas struggled to contain his mirth, forcing his face to be straight as he inspected her from top to toe.

"What are you doing?" Her hands were on her hips and there was a slight outrage on her face. It didn't spoil her beauty one bit, those classic high cheekbones and green eyes which changed colour even as he searched their depths.

"Seaweed."

Her expression altered again. No emotion. Nothing to read, which concerned him more than the earlier outrage.

"I'm not a mermaid, Thomas. When I emerge from the depths, I leave the seaweed where it belongs."

Deep in her eyes was a sparkle.

"Perhaps I'll be the judge of that. When we meet next." He said.

Her chin lifted, and her eyebrows. "You assume a lot."

Thomas shrugged. "Why are you out in the rain, Martha Ryan?"

The fun left her eyes. "Tell me, Thomas Blake, should I leave River's End, move in with my sister to pursue a career other than my real calling? Should I study for years to gain the privilege of teaching other people's children?"

You want to leave? I just found you.

"Is this your idea, or someone else's?" he ventured.

"Mother thinks I must have a real job."

"As opposed to…?"

Martha opened her mouth to answer, then closed it.

"Do you even like children? If you were to be a teacher?" What on earth was he going on about now?

Her smile touched his heart. "I love them. And teaching wouldn't be so bad, but I have…plans. May I see your painting?"

No.

"Yes." Whatever was wrong with him? "It isn't done though. I just started…"

She wasn't listening. Martha stood back enough to see the whole canvas. Her eyes roamed it, her lips flickering then brow furrowing. She must hate it. Thomas stepped to the opening of the alcove to breath.

"Why are you here, Thomas?"

Martha was at his side with her palms outstretched to the sky until pools of rain formed in them.

"By here, do you mean this little cave, or the beach, or—"

"Australia, silly."

Thomas blinked. Where else would he live? Martha angled her hands, so the pools of water transformed into tiny waterfalls.

She caught her watching him and grinned. "It is possible I was a mermaid in another life."

"Where should I live?"

"Paris, of course. Or New York. Isn't Soho all the rage for struggling artists? But France would be my first choice."

"For what?"

Martha leaned against the side of the alcove with her head tilted as if amused by his confusion. "Hold exhibitions. Become a famous artist. Your eye for detail will attract the arty crowd and your…charm, will sell your work."

Thomas laughed.

"I'm serious."

"Martha, you are sweet. And too kind. But what I do barely represents a moment in time with colours that probably ruin it anyway." He turned from the entrance, from Martha. "The rain has eased if you want to go."

Allowing her to see the painting was a mistake. Nobody ever did until he'd finished one if he even showed them to anyone. Most remained unseen. He wasn't some future master. Thomas knew he had talent. Just not the kind to set the world alight.

"I'm not sweet. Not at all." She squeezed the rain from her long ponytail. "I'll go because I know better than to stay where I'm not welcome."

"I didn't say—"

She stalked past Thomas, out onto the wet sand, where she turned to face him. "Your tone of voice said it. Nevertheless, you have a rare talent, and what you should understand about me is I am honest. I never say a thing I don't believe. And I always keep a promise."

He crossed the small distance between them. There was fire in her eyes. With her chin raised and hands on her hips, Martha was formidable.

A little wild. Unpredictable. Mine to tame. A mermaid called Martha.

A smile touched his lips before he could stop it.

"You're laughing at me."

"Not at all. I'm sorry I sounded rude earlier. My frustration is with myself because I am not the artist you assume."

Martha's expression softened. Before Thomas could react, she placed both hands onto his chest and gazed up at him. "Know this, Thomas Blake. I believe in you. So anytime you lose faith, find me."

With that, she was gone, running up the steps. All she left behind were two damp handprints on his T-shirt. And yearning in his soul.

5

OBSERVATIONS

"Today is exactly one month." Martha opened a small picnic basket to extract a thermos, two mugs, and a foil covered plate. These she placed between Thomas and herself on the end of the jetty. "Although this morning the sun is already wide awake."

Clear blue skies accompanied this perfect morning, and although still very early, the air was warm with the promise of summer ahead.

"I love the way you express things." Thomas sat cross-legged, facing her across the small picnic. "The sun is wide awake. Have you considered creative writing?"

Martha avoided his eyes. What she'd always wanted slipped away a little more every day. Even last night, both parents were in unusual agreement Martha should accept one of the offers before it expired. Maybe they had a point.

"You could write children's books." He continued, unaware of course of how sensitive the subject was. She'd not told him her dreams and why would she? One month ago, they'd met. Only one month.

After the way she'd behaved on the beach, putting her hands onto Thomas' chest and telling him he should move to Paris, Martha expected he would keep his distance. She knew she was opinionated, but always managed to keep them to herself, apart from with her family and Frannie, but Thomas brought out the worst in her. How could he not believe in his talent? Once she'd run up the steps that day, she'd glanced back but he was out of sight.

The following day she'd seen Thomas in town. He was carrying shopping bags to an old car with his mother. Martha was following Lilian into the fabric shop and hesitated outside as he crossed the road, taking his mother's elbow to assist her up the kerb. He opened the passenger door for Mrs Blake before loading the shopping into the boot. As he'd gone to the driver's side, he'd smiled at Martha. Had he known she was watching the whole time?

She smiled in return, a pleasant warmth filling her heart. The smile was still in place when she joined Lilian inside, who gave her a curious look before glancing through the window. Only after they left the shop, new fabric ordered for a dress Lilian wanted made, was a comment passed.

"The Blake family are good people, Martha. And stationmasters are a vital link in the success of our business. But they aren't marrying material. Not for a Ryan daughter."

"Mother, I'm only nineteen and have no interest in settling down!"

Or do you?

"I married at nineteen," Lilian huffed. "Much better to have grown children and still be young enough to enjoy the finer things in life."

Martha kept her thoughts on this private but cautioned herself to be more careful around Thomas if her mother was watching. Her sharp eyes missed little and Thomas deserved better than Lilian Ryan's interference.

Besides, they were friends. Nothing more.

"Martha? You are miles away." Thomas touched her arm.

"Oh."

Just friends.

"I was thinking of something my mother said a couple of weeks ago."

"Was it how dark green your eyes are when you are deep in thought?"

"Don't believe she has mentioned my eyes often." Martha busied herself pouring cups of hot chocolate. She knew how he liked it. Seven times they'd met at the café to talk. Not that she was counting.

"Are you planning on sharing what she said?" Thomas accepted the mug. "Thank you."

"There's sugar if you need any." Martha stirred a teaspoon full into her own drink. "She was going on about how she married young. Her children are adults. Which allows her to be young enough now to enjoy the finer things in life. Quote. Whatever that means. All she does is plan dinner parties and pick flowers and keep Palmerston House perfect."

"And she wants you to follow her example?"

Martha shot a glance at Thomas, who watched her over his mug as he sipped. Was he teasing her now?

"According to Mother, there isn't a man between here and Melbourne suitable to marry a Ryan."

Thomas almost lost the mouthful of hot chocolate as he half laughed; half choked. Martha passed him a serviette. She wanted to laugh as well. "Sadly, she believes herself."

After wiping his mouth and putting the mug down, Thomas took Martha's hand. "Sadly? Why, are you planning on go further afield to find a husband."

He'd never held her hand before. Not like this, stroking her palm. Little sparks flew up her arm. Nice sparks. She put her own mug beside his.

"Whatever makes you believe I want a husband?"

"Observations."

Something changed in his face. His eyes drew her in with their intensity. He moved a fraction closer.

"Observations?" Her voice sounded breathless to her ears. How annoying.

"You love children. You're kind. Smart. And funny."

"I…am?"

"And you like people. You don't judge them by class or money."

What does any of this have to do with marriage?

"Martha?"

Thomas was so close now. He played with her hair, brushing it from her face. Martha's heart raced and her stomach fluttered with tiny butterflies.

"Yes?"

"Do you believe in love at first sight?"

The words hung between them.

Martha's tongue touched her lips. Salty lips, from the same sea breeze ruffling Thomas' hair. She wanted to run her fingers through it. But those words he'd asked…

"I believe in it." Thomas touched his lips to hers. "I did the moment we met here. One month ago."

6

ONLY TIME ITSELF

Chisel in one hand and hammer in the other, Thomas concentrated on a small area of the cliff face near the stone steps.

He'd been raised to respect property and the environment. His mother would be horrified at his actions, but she never visited the beach, so it was unlikely she'd discover this. The rock didn't care. It was as old as time and worn smooth by the relentless weather coming off the Great Southern Ocean. Violent storms. Torrential rain. Blistering sun.

My efforts won't harm you.

Soon Martha would arrive, running along the sand to throw herself into his arms. The sun warmed his back as its rays flooded the beach. His stomach growled from missing breakfast, but this was more important than food. He tapped and chipped. Tapped and chipped.

"Whatever are you doing?"

Thomas tossed the tools on the ground, covered his work with a hand and dropped a kiss onto Martha's forehead. "All will be revealed."

"Can I see now?"

"No, my impatient sweetheart. Have you eaten?"

Martha frowned as she stared at his hand on the cliff. "Not yet. Thomas—"

"Martha. I need another few minutes."

"I'll watch. I'll be quiet."

Thomas laughed.

"I will!"

"Instead of us debating, would you mind going to the café? I arranged for apple pies…is it almost eight?"

Martha's eyes lit up. "You did? How thoughtful, Tom." She glanced at her watch. "Will be once we get there."

He gestured with his head. "Have to hold this cliff up for a bit longer."

"Very funny. I'll go. But if you are still holding up the cliff when I return, I shall eat both pies on the steps. Just out of reach." She grinned and stepped a bit too far away as his free arm shot out to bring her in for a kiss.

She skipped away, casting a glance over her shoulder with a smile. He waited until Martha was too far to see his inscription and retrieved the tools.

Every day he learned something new about the beautiful woman who filled his heart with joy. Such a fusion of traits.

Her generosity of spirit was at odds with occasional flashes of self-ishness and pride. Martha had a depth of sensitivity and gentleness which melted him. She'd do anything to protect those she loved. Unless they hurt her feelings. Then, he'd seen a sharp temper emerge. Never his way. Not so far.

And if it does?

The corners of Thomas' lips curved up. Martha could be as stubborn and cross as she wished, but he'd be her rock, always. Strong as this cliff in the face of a hurricane.

Martha returned across the sand, carrying a paper bag and two bottles of juice. Without even looking his way, she climbed a few steps and placed her goods on one, then straightened. "These pies smell divine. I'm sure I can manage both."

With a grin, Thomas chipped out a last fragment and stepped back to view his handiwork. It was good. He held out a hand and Martha tore down the steps. Ignoring him, she peered at the engraving, their initials with a love heart.

She reached out a hand to touch it. "Why does T heart M?"

Thomas smacked her hand—the lightest of touches—before enclosing it in his. "Don't annoy the artist." He tried to sound stern, but Martha grinned at him before cuddling against his chest.

"I love it. You are so clever and so wonderful, Tom."

He wrapped her in his arms and dropped a kiss onto her head. "It will take millennia before this cliff erodes. This way, only time itself can erase our love."

TO CATCH THE BREEZE

At the other end of the beach, a track meandered up the opposite cliff to a broad expanse of meadow. Looking inland, the town of River's End was a pretty toy town and Palmerston House just visible if looking in the right direction.

But Palmerston House was the last place Martha wanted to be today after a full morning of preparing the homestead for her father's big birthday party tonight. She'd slipped away after lunch once all her tasks were completed, longing to see Thomas. Her commitments had stopped them meeting at the jetty, even early.

When she'd told him she'd be busy all day, he'd kissed her—for quite a while—then said he'd spend the day painting from the top of the cliff. And he was here, perched on a collapsible stool at an easel. He wouldn't be expecting company and a little flush of delight warmed her. She'd chosen a pretty white sundress, like the one she was wearing when they'd first met, and her hair fell around her bare shoulders beneath a wide straw hat.

She stopped a few feet from Thomas, looking over his shoulder as he mixed colours on the palette. Did he not know she was there?

Martha picked a daisy and tickled his neck. He brushed it away, so she did it again and this time, he reached up and captured her hand.

She laughed, freed her hand and tossed her hat onto the grass. Martha ran her hand through her hair, letting the strands fall. "I just had to escape Palmerston. Mother is getting the house ready for Father's birthday party, and I simply couldn't bear listening to her going on and on about the guest list!"

"She forgot to add me to it."

"We'll tell them all soon. I don't want to share you with anyone yet." Only Frannie knew. And George, the jeweller's son and Tom's dearest friend. Both were sworn to secrecy.

How gorgeous the ocean is today?

Martha found herself on the edge of the cliff. A place she'd stood a thousand times.

"Be careful," Thomas warned.

It sounded like something her father would say. She was an adult, not some child needing safety lessons.

Martha stretched her arms out. She lifted herself onto her toes, her fingers wide as if to catch the breeze. If she closed her eyes and leaned into the wind...

Strong arms whipped around her waist, startling her into opening her eyes.

"I said to be careful. You could fall." Thomas' tone was nothing like her father's. No, it was thick with concern and there was a definite reprimand there.

"You'd always catch me."

Thomas tightened his grip. "That's not all I'd do."

Her breath caught. What would he do? She wasn't ready to find out so laughed to cover sudden nerves. Not entirely scary ones.

Thomas spun her around to face him, taking a step back from the cliff edge at the same time. His arms were strong, and his eyes bored into hers.

How she loved him. Martha gazed at Thomas. He lowered his mouth to within an inch of hers, and her eyelids fluttered down in anticipation.

"You need someone to curb your wild nature. Someone with a firm hand," he whispered.

Wait on. Kiss me.

Martha opened her eyes. "You can't tame the wind. Or the ocean, except in your paintings."

He released her and returned to the easel.

Martha glared after him, hands on her hips as he picked up a brush. Had he just dismissed her?

Love him she might, but stay where she wasn't welcome, she wouldn't. She swept her hat off the grass and stalked down the hill.

"Bye, Martha."

"Goodbye, Thomas."

She sneaked a glance over a shoulder, and he was smiling at her, then blew a kiss. All the irritation drained away and she blew one back.

8

TOO LONG A SECRET

In the attic of the cottage, Thomas glared at a different canvas. The green hue was wrong again. And the brushstrokes too coarse or even amateurish. He stalked away from the easel and threw the offending paintbrush onto the workbench.

You'll never do her justice. Never.

To gaze into Martha's eyes was to see into her heart.

"How can mere paint reflect perfection?"

He squatted, head in his hands, forcing himself to think rather than react.

This portrait meant everything. Martha had no idea what he was doing and if his insistence on keeping it a secret wasn't so…insistent, she could sit for him and he'd get it right. Or close to right. But this was her Christmas gift. Recreating the colour of her eyes was the most important part of the whole painting.

Thomas straightened, then retrieved the offending paintbrush. He'd paid too much for these to toss them aside, frustrated or not. He cleaned up, his mind still on Martha. Since their first kiss on the jetty transported them from sort-of-friends to a secret couple, his life had new purpose. The hours he worked to support himself and pay board to his parents dragged, yet the minute he was with Martha, time flew past. He couldn't capture it.

Nor the colour of her eyes.

Until he resolved this, he wouldn't rest. He needed to see her.

———

At the gates of Palmerston House, Thomas changed his mind.

Their relationship was between the two of them. Thomas longed for Martha to visit the cottage, have lunch with his parents, show her the paintings no other eyes had seen. He'd ask her opinion on the sea and landscapes ready for sale, should he ever get the courage.

She kept saying no. Not yet. Not until the time is right. And she'd kiss him or snuggle into his arms and he'd bury the pain.

Martha had complained about how busy she'd be over the following weeks. They'd sat on a dune one evening, waiting for the first stars to appear in a velvet sky. "December is Mother's favourite time of year. Christmas begins on the first and she follows every tradition she knows. Even some of Father's Irish traditions."

"I know how generous your parents are at Christmas." Thomas kissed Martha's hand. "Opening Palmerston House to the town for a long lunch. Always a bonus in the pay packet for my father. When do you celebrate?"

"Christmas night. Mother and I set up a small dining room as a Christmas wonderland and it is locked until dinner time. And there is only ever family there."

"Ever? What about friends?"

Martha had looked away, out across the sea, her face unreadable. "I only recall family. And Dorothy may not even be there this year. Four becomes three."

"Or four again. When you bring someone home." Thomas didn't expect an invitation, or anything more than her agreeance of one day. But she'd changed the subject, kissing him until he forgot the conversation.

A week ago, instead of tending bar at the pub, he'd been sent to pour drinks at a private function for the local council. The Ryans were there, seated at a table at the front with business leaders from other local towns. Martha sat between Patrick and a well-dressed man a few years older than Thomas. They chatted constantly, Martha giggling at something the man said. Thomas smiled. He recognised her being the polite and dutiful daughter and making friends along the way.

On his way out of the kitchen, he'd almost collided with Martha and she'd immediately shot a look over her shoulder to the table.

"Nobody saw. And why would anyone care?"

"You don't understand." She whispered. "They can't know. Not yet."

"Sweetheart, I'm a waiter tonight. Just serving drinks. You look beautiful." Her hair was up and make-up perfect.

"Shh. Someone will hear you." Martha's lips curved up for a second, taking the sting from the words and then she was gone, sliding back in her seat as if she'd never left.

Thomas didn't understand jealousy. It wasn't in his nature to envy another person or resent someone else's success. A decent work ethic and a degree of talent was enough to attain almost any dream.

But for a moment, at the ornate gate to Martha's home, he coveted acceptance.

Let me into your life, Martha. Completely.

He dropped his head. Until she was confident of the future, Martha needed his support, not his selfish wishes.

"Tom? Why are you here? Is something wrong?"

Martha appeared along the driveway, hurrying, glancing behind herself. As she had the other night.

It cut into Thomas. "Just leaving. Sorry."

"Wait!" She sprinted the last few steps. "Come and talk to me. Tell me what's up."

"Come where?"

Her hand reached for his, but he stepped back. He wasn't welcome amongst such wealth and status. He never would be good enough for the boss's daughter.

A flash of anger crossed her face. "Thomas Blake. If you've come to break my heart, then let's do this. But not out here!"

She spun toward the house and stalked away.

Break your heart? What about mine?

Enough of the games. She needed to decide. Today.

9

AT THE EDGE OF THE POND

Not sure if Thomas followed, Martha skirted around Palmerston House through the garden. Her parents were away for a few days in Melbourne to see Dorothy and continue Father's birthday celebrations. And Thomas knew they were.

But he also understood her feelings on making their relationship public. Until she found the right time to tell her parents there was a risk of a terrible fallout. Dorothy once liked a local boy, and all it took to end their budding romance was Lilian speaking to his parents.

I won't let her destroy Thomas and me.

His expression was one of defeat. What would bring him here, then upset him so he wouldn't let her touch him?

Behind the house, and its immediate garden, lush greenery led to a massive pond. Not quite a lake despite the ducks and reeds around one side. This was one of her favourite retreats, where the trees offered shade and privacy and the water soothed her no matter what else was wrong.

She stalked to the end of the path and waited near the pond. Out here, no staff would notice Thomas, not unless the gardener was working in the area. And she was at the point where she no longer cared. Their love was either strong enough to stand against her mother or would fail eventually anyway.

"Why am I here, Martha?" Thomas stopped in the middle of the path, arms crossed, feet planted apart. "I wasn't going to intrude."

"Yet, you were at the gates. I saw you stop and stand there. Like you ran into a barrier."

"You are the barrier."

Martha blinked, aware her mouth was open. She closed it.

"Making all the rules. What I can do and say." Such bitterness in his voice.

"I don't understand you—"

"Like the event I waited at. Not allowed to speak to you yet..." Thomas glowered at Martha and then stalked to the edge of the pond. He scooped up a handful of pebbles and skimmed them forcefully, one after another, across the surface of the water.

"You think you're so god-damned irresistible." He ground the words out.

Do you mean me sitting next to that boring man who Father needs money from?

"Sometimes I hate you!" Martha wanted to push him into the pond, but the ducks might not appreciate it.

"Maybe you'll stop following me around."

"Following you around? Everywhere I go, there you are. Even places you're not invited to!"

"Maybe I have to invite myself! I'm hardly suitable for the grand affairs of the Ryan family now, am I?"

"I don't care what my family thinks! I care about what I want."

Nothing matters except you. Nothing. And now I'm losing you.

Thomas tossed the last of the pebbles aside and faced Martha.

Hands on her hips, she needed one more comment, one more wrong look and she'd burst into tears.

Thomas smiled.

"Don't you dare laugh at me!"

"Never. So, what is it you want, Martha Ryan, she who only cares about what she wants?"

"I want to travel the world. I want to be a famous writer. I want to…" her words trailed off as Thomas came close enough to touch her. She expected him to, but he did not.

"Go on."

"Um, I want the freedom to do whatever I want. With nobody telling me what to do."

Not even you.

"Nobody? That might be a lonely life, sweetheart."

"I'll…I'll take lovers when it suits me."

Thomas brushed the hair back from her eyes. "No, you won't."

"You can't stop me." He could. He had to. She wanted no other man now or ever.

"You don't get to choose who you fall in love with. Do you?" Thomas brushed his lips against Martha's. "Do you, Martha?"

With a shuddering sigh, Martha melted against him. It was time to stop hiding this love from the world.

10

WHAT LIES AHEAD

Christmas was the best Thomas ever had. His parents, although sceptical for the future of the couple, welcomed Martha. They'd invited her to enjoy a Christmas Eve feast and even given her a set of handkerchiefs embroidered by Thomas' mother.

Martha's family were less accommodating. Patrick said little but Lilian was openly incensed. There was no invitation to any part of the festivities at Palmerston House, and Lilian made it clear he wasn't to attend the open house lunch with his parents.

"I'm beyond angry with Mother!" Martha's outrage had warmed Thomas' heart even as it worried him.

"Sweetheart, she's still your mother and getting between you is not my intention."

A compromise was reached. Martha helped with the lunch, then had the afternoon to spend with Thomas before returning for the dinner-for-three. They'd cuddled in the alcove in the cliff during the hot afternoon, sharing a bottle of homemade lemonade and slices of traditional Christmas cake from the kitchen of Palmerston House.

"She'll get used to you. Eventually." Martha said.

"And if she doesn't?"

"Then she'll miss getting to know the most incredible man on the planet."

"Who?"

"Funny." Martha kissed him, then settled back in his arms. "All I want is to be with you, Tom. No more study. Father says there's a job in the office at the mill, so I shall work part time and write part time. Until my first publishing deal, of course."

"What does Lilian say about this arrangement?"

"She doesn't know yet."

Thomas straightened despite a grumble from Martha. He took her face in his hands. "There is no chance she will accept it, is there?"

"But she will live with it. Anyway, she's talking about going to Ireland with Father for a visit in a few months."

After a kiss, Thomas stood and stretched. "His homeland."

"They have friends living there. Probably family I know nothing about. And an old estate. The point is she has something new to plan for. Once she sees how happy we are, she'll deal with it."

"And are we?"

He offered a hand and Martha let him pull her to her feet.

"Happy?" she asked, eyes dancing with the answer.

Thomas nodded, lifting her hand to his lips.

"Depends if you like having me around. Pretty sure I'm out of the will so unless I write a bestseller—"

"*When* you write one, or two. Or three."

"And when you sell so many paintings the attic is empty—"

"Money doesn't matter to me, Martha. Never has. Never will. I'm never going to have a big house or staff."

Martha rose onto her toes to touch her lips to his. "Then we truly are happy. Give me a cottage near the sea, somewhere to write, and love. Not one thing more."

"No pets?"

"I would love a dog and a cat. Walk me back?" Martha checked her watch with a sigh.

Hand in hand they followed the tideline on the hard, cooler sand, waves covering their feet.

"Let me understand your future needs." Thomas said. "A cottage with somewhere to write. Love. A dog. A cat."

"Oh. And a garden to grow vegetables and an orchard."

"This list is growing."

"And our friends. Frannie adores you and I love George...as a friend, of course."

"Of course."

"And we will travel. How else will Paris meet their next artist of choice?"

Still debatable.

By the time they reached the gates of Palmerston House, Martha's list was a mile long. Inheritance or not, a life with Martha would fill his heart with love and laughter. He watched her hurry down the driveway until she waved from the steps of the house, her kiss fresh on his lips. Would she really leave all of this behind when he followed his heart and proposed?

11

A MOMENT IN TIME

"Father won't do anything to support my choices, Frannie. I just need him to help make Mother understand." Elbows on the café table, chin on her hands, Martha was at her wit's end.

Frannie Williams filled her mouth with half a cupcake and nodded in sympathy.

"Ever since my birthday, Mother won't stop reminding me of my duty to the Ryan family. Dorothy taking the trainee manager's job in the city has added to her woes and somehow this is all my fault!"

"Do you think she'd be happier if you changed your mind about being a teacher? Don't screw your nose up!" Frannie giggled and stirred her tea. "Think of it like this. You do what she wants for a little bit. Get your teaching degree or whatever it is, and by then she'll have been to Ireland and come home. She and your dad will probably retire, and she'll be mellowed. Ready for grandchildren."

Heat spread up Martha's neck. Babies with Thomas was something on her mind. Not now, not for a couple of years and anyway, he hadn't even proposed. But she dreamed about it.

"Frannie, if I'm away for two years, or three, can't remember how long it takes, how will our relationship survive?"

"We'll always be friends."

Martha smiled and sat back. "Not us, silly. I know we will."

"You mean Thomas?" Frannie shrugged. "Doesn't true love last forever?"

She was right. It did and it would. Martha played with the pendant she wore. Tom's gift for her twentieth birthday. A love heart entwined with their initials, just like the one he'd carved into the cliff face.

"What would you do, Frannie?"

"Marry Tom."

"Sorry?"

"If you really love him, then marry him. Forget about what anyone else wants."

Since when were you so selfish? But you have a point.

Frannie picked up the other half of the cupcake. "Am I still taking photos of you both this afternoon?"

Mid-winter in River's End was often mild compared to inland towns. Today, though, was blustery and cold enough for Martha to throw a jacket over her dress. The wind whipped her hair around as she and Thomas wandered toward the lagoon, hand in hand.

"Um, aren't we meant to be taking photos?" Frannie called out from a distance behind. She loved photography and had a new camera to test.

Martha stopped to let Frannie catch up, but Thomas kept walking.

"Tom? Frannie's taking our photo!"

He glanced back. He'd told Martha when they got to the beach, he'd wanted to talk to her about something important, and Frannie's appearance at the last moment was met with less enthusiasm than Martha expected.

A few photos, then we'll find somewhere out of the wind to talk.

Martha struck a pose for Frannie. "He's so rude! Just take my photo, 'cos I'm better looking than him."

In what she hoped was a dramatic pose, Martha gazed off into the distance while Frannie played with the focus on the camera.

Her thoughts were miles away when Thomas grabbed her around the waist. She squealed and tried to escape but he wrestled her onto the sand.

"Thomas Blake, let me go! Oh, there's sand in my hair now!" Martha pushed against his arms as he laughed and held her even tighter. "It's not funny!"

He must have thought it was as he kissed her until she stopped struggling. As soon as she relaxed, Thomas let her go, stood, and extended his hand.

Martha ignored him and climbed to her feet, making a big deal of shaking the sand off her clothes and out of her hair.

"Stubborn girl." Thomas said.

His laugh followed her as she stomped away. She heard Frannie tell him off. "You shouldn't do that! She's sensitive."

About to laugh at such silliness, Martha heard Thomas running after her and sped up. She made it to the stone steps at the same time he did. There was such happiness in his eyes she couldn't stay cross.

Martha sat on Tom's lap as he told her of a rumour about the train line. The government was changing the rail gauge, not for the first time, but unless the timber mill was prepared to pour a lot of money into an upgrade, the line would close next year.

"I don't know what to make of it. I wonder if this is making my mother so upset and she is taking it out on us?" Martha played with the pendant. "What will your parents do?"

"They have a retirement plan. This will free me from the pressure to take over the role. Martha, this may be our opportunity."

The wind dropped and the sun emerged. So did Frannie, panting as she floundered in the sand. "Quick. I can get a perfect shot with the sea behind you."

Martha's heart raced. What would happen to Palmerston House? And River's End? How would it continue without the revenue and work provided by the mill?

Thomas positioned them both near the water, backs to it as

Frannie directed. He wrapped his arms around Martha and the panic seeped away.

"This town will survive, sweetheart. And we will have everything we want. Trust me." Thomas whispered to Martha, as though he had read her mind.

"Now, smile!"

12

OUR JETTY. ALWAYS

One year from the day they met, Thomas invited Martha to the jetty for a breakfast picnic. At least, he told her it was a picnic, then forgot to bring anything. He was early and paced the length of the jetty wondering if he had time to find some food. Coffee, seeing as they'd both taken up the habit over winter.

What if he was gone too long and she left before he returned? No. Not today. They could eat later. Go to the café and buy the most elaborate breakfast to celebrate.

What if she says no?

Halfway along the timber boards, Thomas halted. Surely, she would say yes. Of course, she would. This was nervousness.

Did I bring it?

His hand flew to his shirt pocket, reassured by the small bulge there. Calm down.

For the past week he'd kept busy with extra hours at the hotel. Anything to pass the time and avoid being too close to Martha because he was as likely to give away his secret too soon. A secret between him and George.

For George was the maker of the two most beautiful rings Thomas had ever seen. Unlike Thomas who was reluctant to embrace his father's career for himself, George followed his predecessors with great joy. The jewellery shop was an icon in River's End and George its next master jeweller. It was with George's gentle nudge he now stood here as the first rays of sunlight touched the sea. "There never will be a wedding if you don't ask Martha to marry you." His friend said as he gifted Thomas the rings.

She was here.

Her hair swung in a ponytail as she sprinted to the jetty. She stopped on the sand at the end of the jetty and waited as Thomas met her.

"Before you say anything, I need to ask something." Martha bit her lip as she looked past him to the far end, where a picnic should be waiting.

"I'm listening."

"I know you've had more work this week, but I wondered if I've done something...said something to upset you."

"Not a thing." He extended a hand and she took it. "Will you join me at the far end?"

"Very formal!" Martha stepped onto the jetty. "You've seemed distracted lately. Is it a painting?"

"I have to admit there is a painting which is impossible to finish. Almost a year old and still, parts of it are beyond my ability to perfect."

"The one you keep under a sheet in the attic?"

"The very one."

Water lapped against the pylons at the end of the jetty. There was little else to hear, but Thomas' heart pounded in his ears.

"Was I meant to bring the picnic?" Martha glanced down. "Shall we sit?"

"I forgot. I was bringing it and I forgot. No. You can't sit." He knelt on one knee.

Martha burst into laughter. "You don't...need to...beg forgiveness." The laughter stopped as his hand slipped into his pocket.

His fingers fumbled.

"Thomas?"

There, he had it.

He took her left hand in his. "One year ago, I found you at this spot and was so annoyed. It was my jetty. My quiet place. And then you smiled and made space for me."

Martha's other hand was at her lips. They quivered. Tears glistened in those gorgeous green eyes and Thomas gulped. If she said no…

"Since then, you've made space for me everywhere in your life. And shown me a quiet place is possible for two…if the right people are in it. Martha Ryan, you are the love of my life. Will you marry me?"

Tears slipped down her cheeks as she nodded. "Yes. Oh, yes, Tom!"

As he stood, she threw her arms around him and he almost lost his balance. His fingers tightened around the ring which he'd yet to put on her hand and for a second he feared it would fall into the sea.

Then he righted himself and kissed her thoroughly and later, after he dried her tears, he fitted the solitaire on her finger. When they married, the ring would be joined by a band of gold, inscribed *Forever Taming the Wind*.

As he would spend the remainder of his life trying to do.

13

AND SO, IT BEGINS

"Y̶ou will not marry him! I forbid it." Lilian sobbed into her hands.

"And yet, I will." Martha was calm. She'd stayed composed throughout Lilian's tirade about the Blake family, Martha's lack of good judgement, and not caring for her mother's feelings. At this point, she was uncertain if she did care about them.

"Your father is telling Dorothy to come home and reason with you. He's in the city right now!"

"Which won't change anything, even if she tried." Martha sighed and flopped next to Lilian on the sofa. "Mother, please stop this. I love you."

"Then call the wedding off."

"We've not set a date for it yet. We will though before the engagement party."

Lilian's head shot up. "Which I will not attend."

"I hope you change your mind. We'd prefer you are part of our lives."

"You've forced me out. You and this boy."

Martha got to her feet. "Enough, Mother. Thomas is a man, a

wonderful, kind man and you should be happy for me." She left the room, unable to bear another round of arguments.

After climbing the sweeping stairway, Martha visited Dorothy's bedroom. This was kept ready for her even though she was clear about only returning on holidays and for special occasions. She'd never live in Palmerston House again.

"I need to be more like you."

Martha sat on the bed and plucked a doll from the open trunk at its end. Dorothy used to sing to her dolls. Line them up on the bed and pretend they were her audience.

What would you do? How would you deal with Mother?

What her older sister did was move. Leave the little town Martha loved so much and find her own life in Melbourne. Thomas was open to travel, so they'd spend some time away after the wedding. When they returned, Mother would be accustomed to having a son-in-law, even one she didn't approve of. And when there were grandchildren, she'd turn back into the mother she remembered before Dorothy left, the one who spoilt her second daughter.

The doll back in the trunk, Martha left the room as she found it with a soft, "Thanks."

True to her word, Lilian refused to attend the engagement party. Even Dorothy couldn't persuade her. Martha hadn't expected her sister to drop everything to travel all the way home for the night, yet she had arrived in the morning and spent almost the whole day comforting their mother.

Patrick gave up asking, pleading, and promising not to drink if she attended. He apologised to Martha every time their paths crossed during the day, and then when he wandered into the hall Thomas had hired.

"She'll come round, ye'll see." He kissed Martha's cheek, shook Thomas' hand, and found a glass of whiskey.

The hall filled with their friends. Music and laughter swept away the last of Martha's sadness about her mother. This was their night, and nothing would spoil it.

George made announcements, Frannie kept the food table stocked, and Dorothy accepted a dance with Patrick.

The music slowed and Thomas enfolded Martha in his arms. "Enjoying this, sweetheart?"

"I think everyone's enjoying themselves."

"Your sister has a new friend." Thomas rotated Martha to see.

Frannie and Dorothy sat near the table, chatting.

"They know each other. Everyone does." Martha said.

"I didn't know you. Not really."

"And now you do?"

Thomas answered by kissing Martha. "Now I do."

"I'm so happy, Tom. So happy I was on the jetty that morning."

They'd overcome whatever twists and turns were ahead. She knew this with every breathe in her body. "I love you, Thomas Blake."

"And I love you, Martha Ryan. Nothing will ever come between us. This, I promise."

Content, Martha leaned her head against his chest, listening to Thomas' steady heartbeat. "I do believe." She whispered. "I do believe in love at first sight." His arms tightened. This love would never be over between them.

ALSO BY PHILLIPA NEFRI CLARK

Christie Ryan Romantic Mysteries series

The Stationmaster's Cottage

Jasmine Sea

The Secrets of Palmerston House

The Christmas Key

Martha

Charlotte Dean Mysteries

The Christmas Tree Thief

Deadly Falls

Deadly Secrets

Doctor Grok's Peculiar Shop Paranormal Shorts

Colony

Table for Two

Wishing Well

ABOUT THE AUTHOR

Phillipa lives just outside a beautiful town in country Victoria, Australia. She also lives in the many worlds of her imagination and stockpiles stories beside her laptop.

Apart from her family, Phillipa's great loves include the ocean, music, reading, the garden, and animals of all kinds.

Please stay in touch for the latest books and news.

www.phillipaclark.com

Printed in Poland
by Amazon Fulfillment
Poland Sp. z o.o., Wrocław

64197679R00033